Peppa's New Friend

Adapted by Michael Petranek

SCHOLASTIC INC.

This book is based on the TV series *Peppa Pig*. *Peppa Pig* is created by Neville Astley and Mark Baker.
Peppa Pig © Astley Baker Davies Ltd/Entertainment One UK Ltd 2003.

ISBN 978-1-338-54590-6

10 9 8 7 6 5 4 3 2 1   19 20 21 22 23
Printed in the U.S.A.   40

First printing 2019
Book design by Mercedes Padró and Two Red Shoes Design

Peppa and her friends are
drawing pictures at school.

Then someone new arrives.

"Children, today we have a visitor," Madame Gazelle says.

The visitor's name is Mandy Mouse.
If Mandy Mouse likes the playgroup,
she will come every day.

All the children say hello.

"I'm Peppa Pig!" says Peppa.
"We're drawing pictures."

Mandy draws her own picture.
"That's really good!" says Peppa.

At playtime, all of the
children race down the hill.

Mandy is very fast.

"Why do you have a wheelchair?"
Peppa asks.

"Because my legs don't work,"
Mandy says. "But I get around
fine! *Squeak!*"

Outside, the children decide
to play basketball.

The team that gets the ball
through the hoop wins!

Mandy catches the ball
and wheels very fast.

She passes the ball to Gerald.
He throws the ball into the hoop.
Their team wins!
Everyone has lots of fun.

Soon playtime is over.

The children hurry back inside.

The hill back to the school
is very big.
"Can I help you?" Peppa asks
Mandy.
"I can do it myself," Mandy says.
"But it is a big hill."

Peppa pushes Mandy
up the hill.

"Thank you, Peppa," Mandy says. "I could do it on my own, but it's easier with two."

Back inside, the parents arrive
to pick up the children.

"So, Mandy," Madame Gazelle
says. "Would you like to come
every day?"

"Yes, please!" Mandy says.
Everyone cheers.

Mandy Mouse loves her new friends. And her new friends love Mandy Mouse!